MARLO

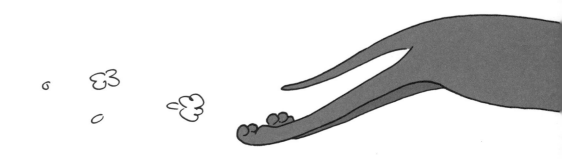

To Mom and Dad,
for reading to me every night and
encouraging me to play in the woods every day

See if you can spot Duck in the pages
of his underwater adventure.

Balzer + Bray is an imprint of HarperCollins Publishers.

Marlo

Copyright © 2017 by Christopher Browne

All rights reserved. Manufactured in China.

No part of this book may be used or reproduced in any manner whatsoever without written permission except in the case

of brief quotations embodied in critical articles and reviews. For information address HarperCollins Children's Books,

a division of HarperCollins Publishers, 195 Broadway, New York, NY 10007.

www.harpercollinschildrens.com

ISBN 978-0-06-244113-3

The artist used pen and watercolor on paper, colored digitally to create the illustrations for this book.

Typography by Dana Fritts

16 17 18 19 20 SCP 10 9 8 7 6 5 4 3 2 1

First Edition

MARLO

Christopher Browne

BALZER + BRAY

An Imprint of HarperCollinsPublishers

On Tuesday morning,
Marlo's owner said,
"Marlo! You're a mess!"

Marlo knew what that meant.

A BATH!

Marlo really didn't like baths.

Luckily, he had Duck
to keep him company.

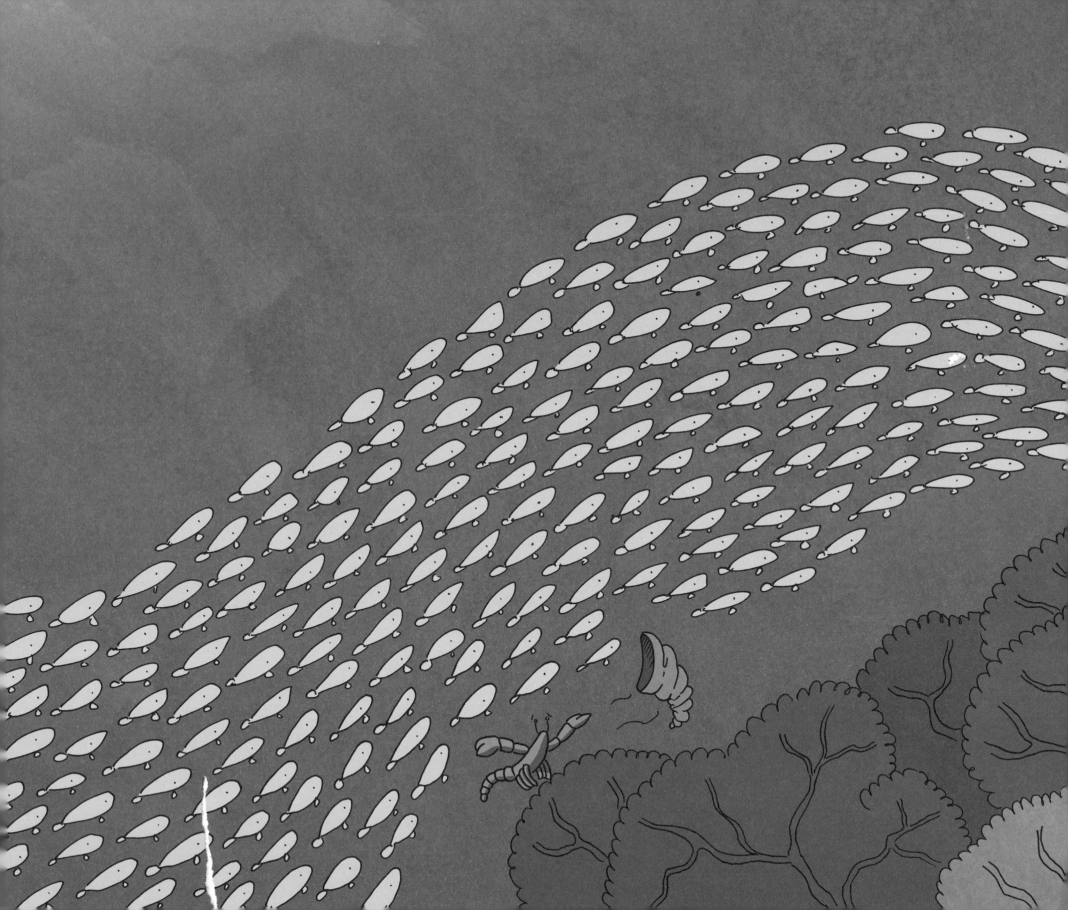

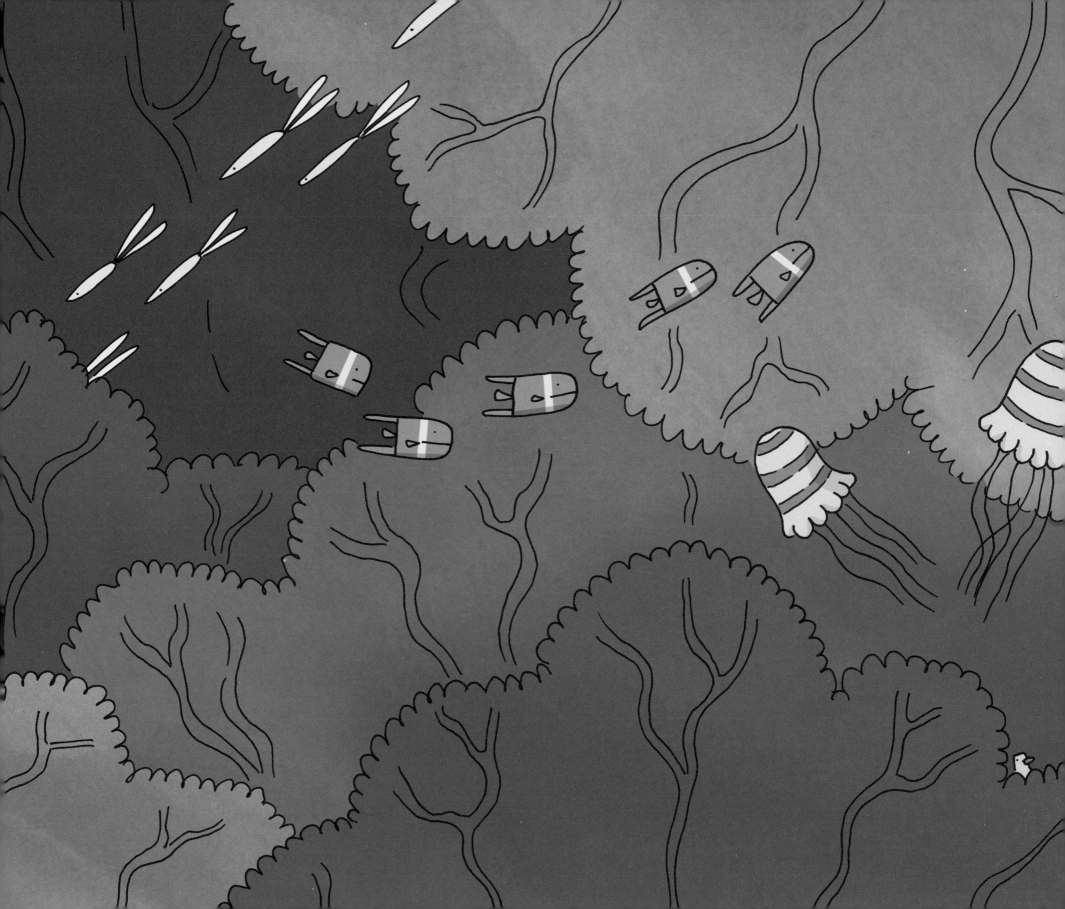

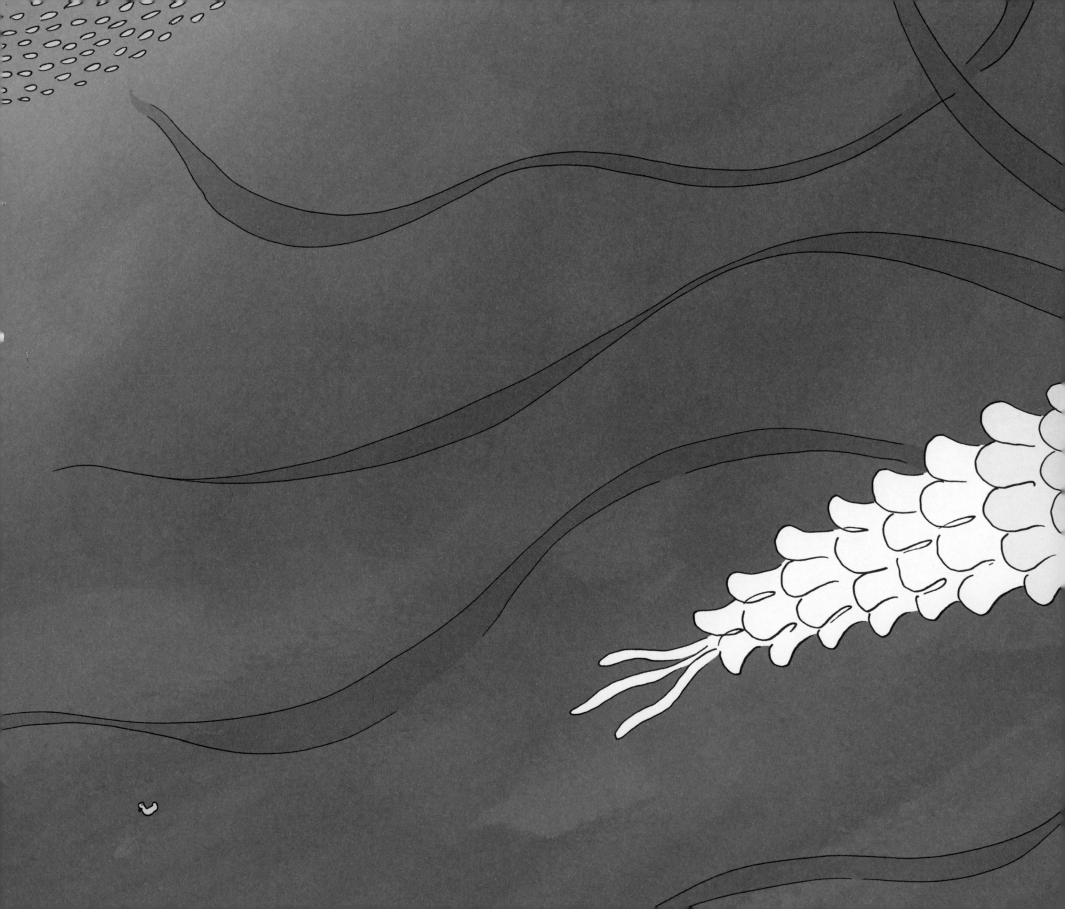

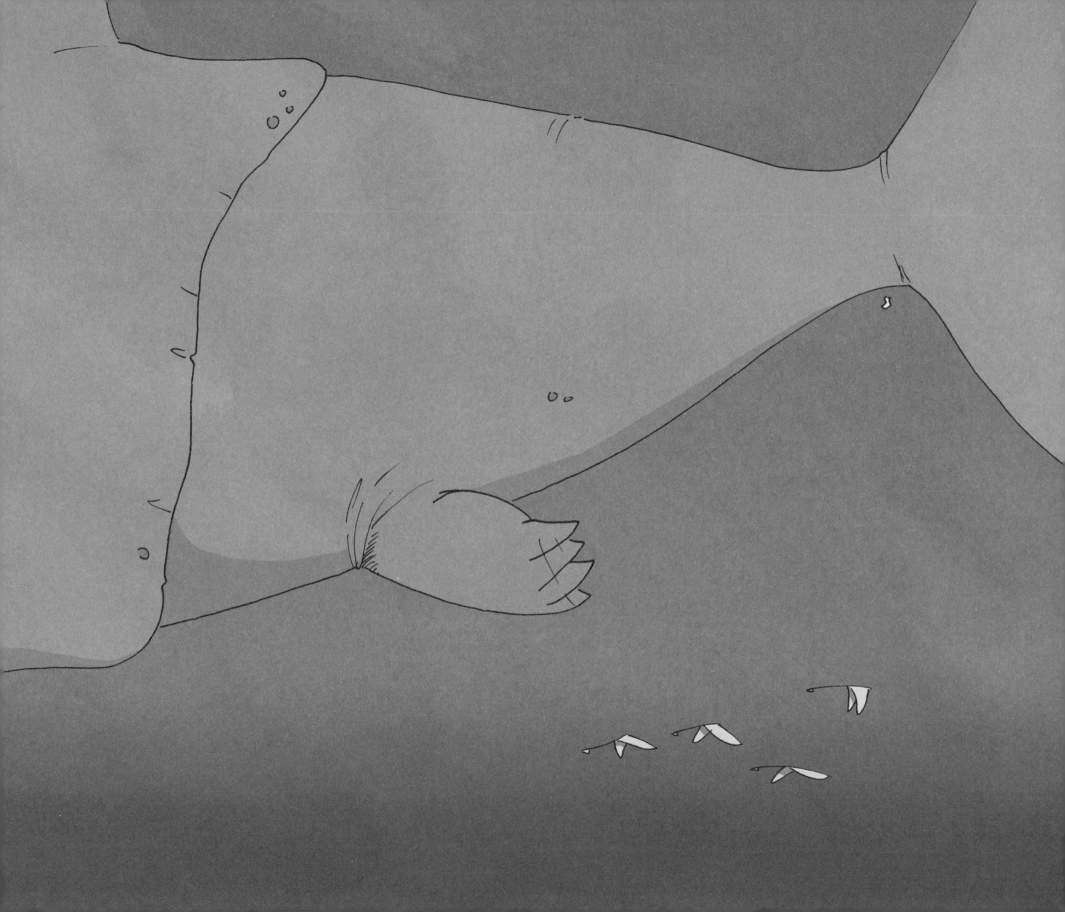

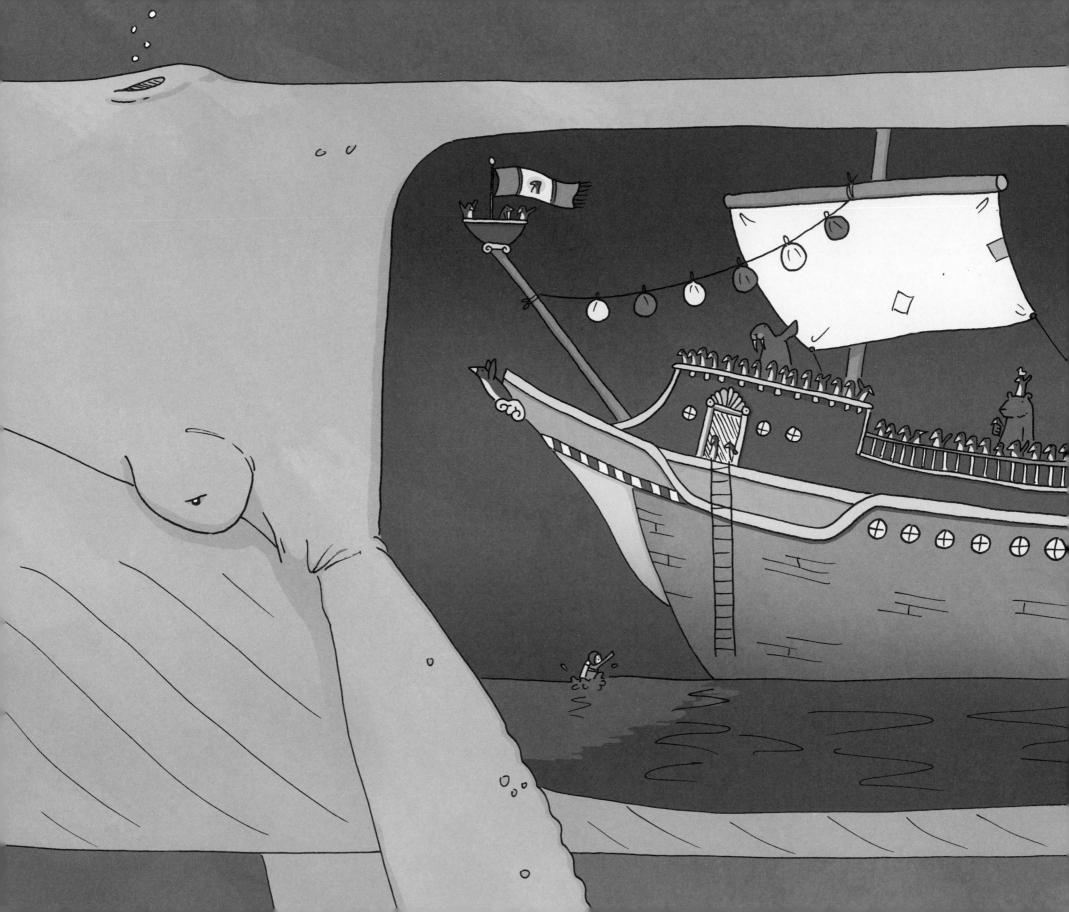

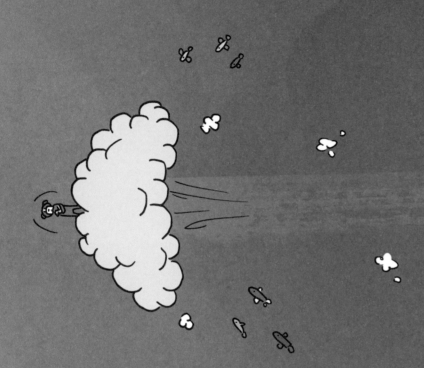

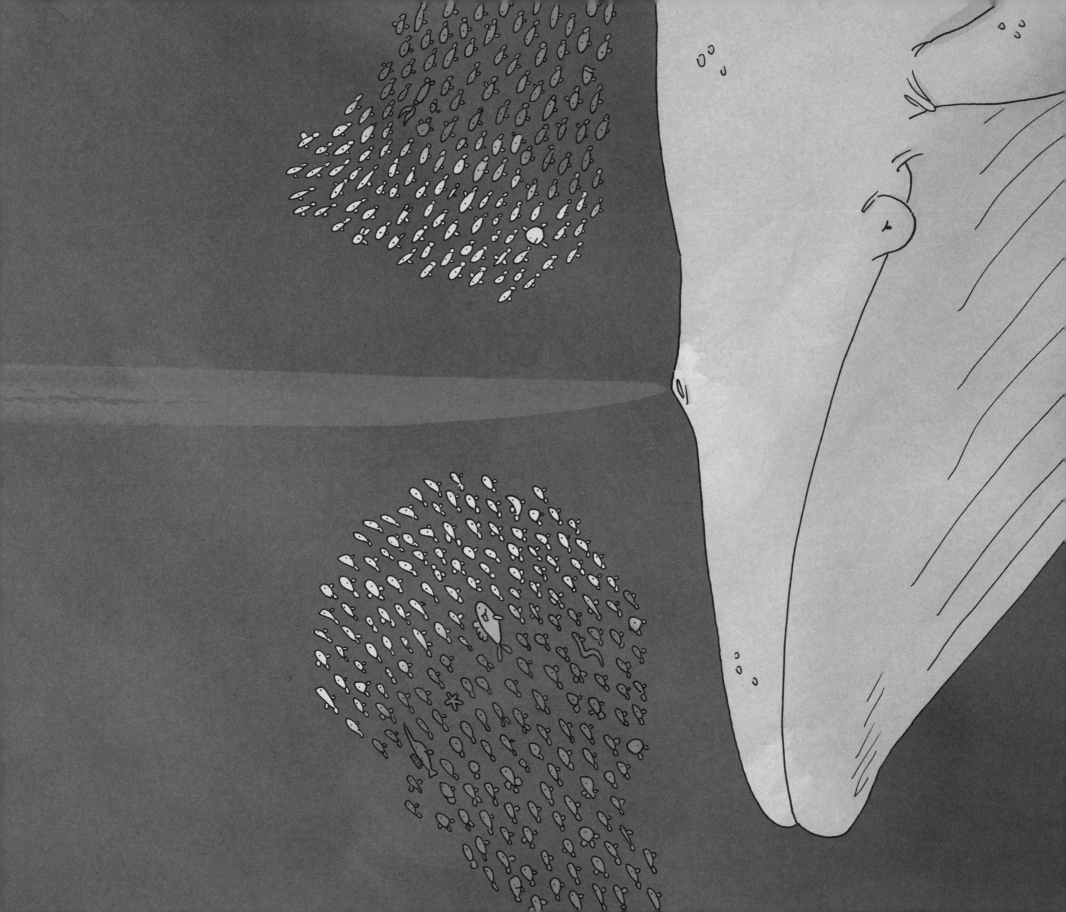

"Marlo? It's time to
get out of the bath."